Give your child
MUPPET™ PIC

Starring the Muppets!

Kermit

Fozzie

Dear Parent,

Now children as young as preschool age can have the fun and satisfaction of reading a book all on their own.

In every Muppet Picture Reader, there are simple words, rebus pictures, and 24 flash cards to cut out and keep. (There is a flash card for every rebus picture plus extra cards for reading practice.) After children listen to each story a couple of times, they will be ready to try it all by themselves.

Collect all the titles in our Muppet Picture Reader series. Once children have mastered these books, they can move on to Levels 1, 2, and 3 in our All Aboard Reading series.

ISBN 0-448-41553-4   A B C D E F G H I J

A MUPPET™ PICTURE READER

Fozzie's Bubble Bath

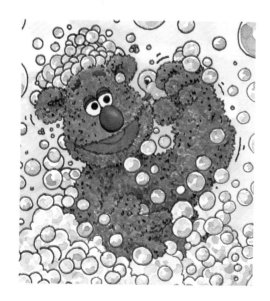

Written by Stuart Bergen
Illustrated by Rick Brown

MUPPET PRESS
Grosset & Dunlap • New York

Ding-dong.

The  – 🔔 rang.

"Who is it?" 🐸 asked.

"It is 🐻.

I am blue."

4

" , do you mean

you are sad?" said.

 opened the .

"No,"  said.

"I am really blue."

 held up a

and .

"I just painted my ."

"You need a bath,"

 told  .

"If you say so,"

 said.

 went into

's  .

He went up the  .

He found the  .

"See you later, ,"
 told .

Then he closed

the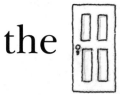

and filled the .

"Oh, ," called .

"Where is the ?"

"The  is on

the ,"

 said.

"Thanks," said.

got in the .

He made lots of .

"Oh, ," called .

"Where is your

rubber ?"

"My rubber

is on the ,"

 said.

 put the

in the  .

"  baths are fun!"

 said.

At last,  was done.

"Oh, ," called .

"Now I need a ."

"A is on the ,"

 said.

"Thanks,"  said.

 got the .

He dried his

and his

and everything

in between.

 opened the 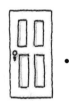 .

"Thanks, ,"

said  .

"That was fun.

And I am not

blue anymore."

But everything else was!

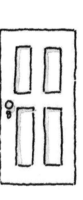

Kermit	bell
door	Fozzie
paint	brush

house	wagon
bathtub	stairs
soap	alligator

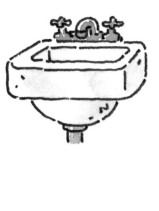

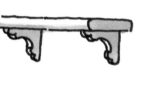

bubbles	sink
shelf	duck
nose	towel

fish	toes
car	boat
book	tree